BUG BUDDIES

Tunnel Trouble

JOE MILLER

Illustrated by Duncan Smith

HarperCollins *Children's*

Spinner's Wood
is full of sticky mud, tall trees
and long grass. But most of
all, it's full of bugs! Now, some
people think that bugs are pests.
But they haven't met Gonzo or
the **Bug Buddies** – four best
friends called **Zap, Buzz,
Lurch** and **Crunch**. Their life
would be perfect if it wasn't
for a spider called **Spinner**,
who has eight legs and one
mission: to trap the whole wood
in his evil web. But you'll
soon find out that even
bugs can be heroes...

Contents

Contents

Chapter 1   9

Chapter 2   22

Chapter 3   33

Chapter 4   45

Chapter 5   56

Chapter 6   66

Chapter 7   73

Chapter 8   82

Bug Facts   90

CHAPTER 1

Zap tingled with excitement as he hovered above the starting twig. Wizzy the horsefly was lined up next to him, buzzing.

"OK," said Crunch, the stag beetle. "First one to Gonzo's Rock and back wins. **Ready... steady...**

GO!" Crunch swiped his antlers down.

The race was on!

Zap flapped his wings with all his might. Spinner's Wood became a green blur as he sped around the rock. He may have been just a tiny weevil, but he felt as tall as a tree when he was flying.

Zap did a loop-the-loop as he soared across the finish line. He'd won! *I'm the fastest bug in the wood,* he thought. *Maybe I'm the fastest bug ever!*

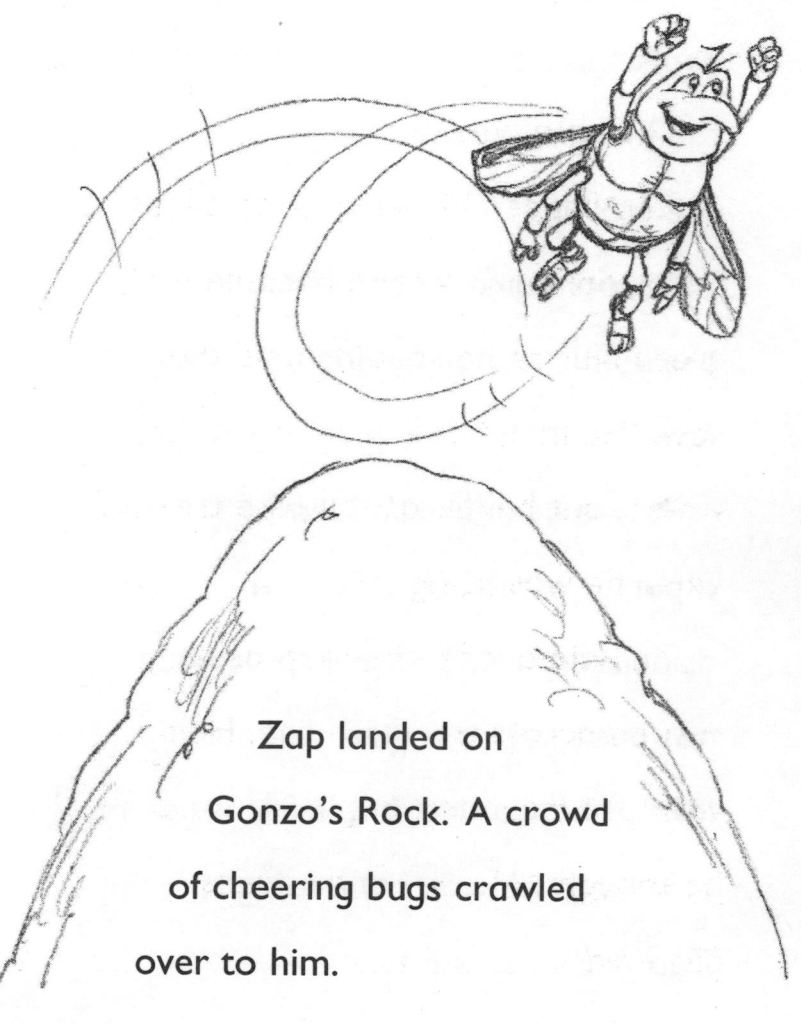

Zap landed on
Gonzo's Rock. A crowd
of cheering bugs crawled
over to him.

11

"Well done," said Crunch, patting him on the back with his claw. Buzz the ladybird nudged his way through the crowd.

"Super flying, champ," he said. "I bet you're up for having this party now."

It had been Buzz's idea to throw a party to celebrate Spinner's disappearance. The evil spider had not been seen since he fell into a lake of honey and Zap's friends were convinced he was gone for good. But Zap wasn't so sure...

Buzz crawled up on to a large stone.

"OK, everyone," he said loudly. "Time to play Guess My Spots!"

Zap smiled. This was the ladybird's favourite game. A group of bugs gathered round. Mazie the millipede crawled forward first and looked at Buzz's back.

"Easy!" she said. "You've got eight spots."

"Buzz," warned Zap, "stop cheating."

The weevil pointed to a tiny speck of blackberry stuck to Buzz's shell, which made it look like he had an extra spot! Buzz flicked his shell and caught the berry-speck in his mouth.

"I didn't see that there," he said, innocently chewing the berry. "Shame to waste it, though!"

Zap and Mazie laughed. Eating was his other favourite thing!

Zap's best friend, Lurch the dung beetle, rushed over pushing a ball of poo.

"Hey, guys," he said. "Fancy
playing Pass the Dung Ball?
Whoever's holding it when the bees
stop humming gets to take a bite!"

"Yuck!" said Buzz, backing away.

"That's one thing even *I* won't eat."

"And that's one game I don't want to win," Zap whispered to Buzz, grinning.

Finally, the party was over. As the last guest crawled away, Gonzo, the wise old grasshopper, hopped on to his rock.

"Well, did you all have fun?" he asked.

"Lots!" said Buzz.

"It's my lucky day," said Lurch. "I won Pass the Dung Ball every time!"

"Thanks for letting us have the party here," said Zap.

"You're welcome," replied Gonzo, smiling.

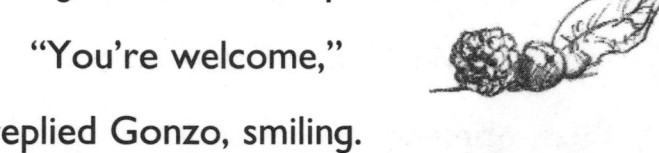

Buzz gave a big yawn. "Having fun makes me sleepy."

Zap looked around — berries and leaves were scattered everywhere. "I think we'd better tidy up first," he said.

Gonzo gave Zap a nod of approval.

"I'll tidy up all the berries," said Buzz,

scuttling towards
a juicy red
mound.

Crunch laughed.
"Don't you mean *eat
all the berries?*"

"Same difference!" yelled Buzz,
through a mouthful.

Zap was dragging the leaves into
a pile when he noticed something
thin and shiny in the bushes. *Was that
spider's silk?* He quickly flew over to
check. **Phew!** It was only a stray
piece of shell left over from a

butterfly chrysalis.

Gonzo hopped over to him. "Stop worrying," said the grasshopper. "Spinner's gone."

"How can you be sure?" asked Zap.

"We've searched the whole wood," replied Gonzo. "There's no sign of him."

Zap nodded, feeling safer. He flew back to Gonzo's Rock.

Once the rock was tidy, the Bug Buddies settled down for the night next to Algae Pond. Zap quickly fell

asleep. He dreamt he was trying to fly, but his wings wouldn't work and he fell into a deep hole. It was pitch black, apart from eight eyes staring at him from the darkness...

Zap woke with a start. *Stop being silly,* he told himself, *it was just a*

dream. He looked up at the dark swaying trees. Was Spinner still out there somewhere?

CHAPTER 2

Zap spent the morning flying around
Spinner's Wood, checking for webs.
He didn't find any, but he still had a
twisty feeling in his tummy. His
nerves faded when he remembered
he had Beetle Ball practice today.
Zap loved playing Beetle Ball – it

was where he got to show off his super-speedy skills! And it was perfect for taking his mind off Spinner.

The Bug Buddies flew over to the practice field and landed next to Gonzo, who was their coach.

"OK, team," said the grasshopper. "I'm going to teach you some new goal-scoring moves. Zap, you go first. Crunch will be goalkeeper."

Gonzo began using his front legs to roll the grass seed ball to Zap.

He was about to knock it forward when he heard a shuffling sound behind him. He turned around to see a family of green tiger beetles enter the clearing. Each beetle was pushing a small egg in front of it, the same way Lurch pushed poo. Zap's wings trembled – with their hard green bodies and dark eyes they looked really scary. And he knew they liked

to eat weevils!

Zap stood up as tall as he could, determined not to look afraid.

The largest of the tiger beetles stood before Gonzo. "My name's Snap," he said. "I need to talk to you about—"

"What are you playing?"

interrupted a young tiger beetle, nudging the grass seed ball with his nose. He looked at the Bug Buddies curiously.

"We were about to play Beetle Ball," said Lurch.

"What's Beetle Ball?" asked the young tiger beetle.

"It's a game," said Buzz, sounding surprised.

Lurched waved his wings. "Come on, we'll show you," he said.

Zap's antennae drooped – he wasn't sure about playing with tiger

beetles. He might get eaten!

"That's a great idea," said Gonzo, looking straight at Zap. "It'll help us all get to know each other."

"Just one game while I talk to the grasshopper," Snap told the young tiger beetles. "We're in a hurry, remember?"

Zap's heart thudded nervously. *I'll run at top speed all the time,* he thought. *That way they'll never catch me!*

Gonzo made a loud clicking sound and the game began. Buzz threw the grass seed down the field. Zap

smiled as he whizzed after it – *that ball was his*. But then a tiger beetle zoomed in front of him and grabbed it! Zap was amazed. No one had

ever overtaken him before! He was
so stunned, he ran straight into
Crunch.

"Sorry," said Zap.

"That's OK," smiled Crunch. "It's
usually me bumping into things!"

Zap steadied himself and
then sprinted with all of
his might. But he
couldn't catch up
with the tiger beetle.
He couldn't catch up
with *any* of them. They
were **super fast.**

They were so speedy; they had to
keep stopping to check they were
going in the right direction!

The match finally ended nil-nil.

"What a game," said Buzz, out of
breath. "Our team couldn't get the
ball and the tiger beetles kept
zooming right past the goal!"

"We'll have to come up with some
special moves if we play them again,"
said Lurch. "They're *so* fast…"

Zap was no longer the fastest bug
in Spinner's Wood. *Oh well,* he thought,
at least they didn't try to eat me!

Crunch, Buzz, Lurch and the young tiger beetles crawled off to find some refreshing sap, but Zap stayed with Gonzo and Snap. He wanted to know what the tiger beetles were up to. After all, it was the job of the Bug Buddies to help protect Spinner's Wood.

"We've come to ask for your help," said Snap. "Our home was invaded by red army ants." He pointed to the eggs they had brought with

them. "And we urgently need somewhere safe to burrow tunnels for our eggs because they are about to hatch! Please can you help us find somewhere in Spinner's Wood?"

Zap's antennae sprang up. The last new arrivals to the wood had stolen honey from the bees and led trusting bugs straight to Spinner! Were the tiger beetles out to trick them too?

CHAPTER 3

"Yes," said Gonzo. "Of course we'll help you."

Zap couldn't believe it. *Has Gonzo forgotten strangers mean danger?* he wondered.

Snap scuttled over to the other tiger beetles to tell them the good news.

"Are you sure about this?" Zap whispered to Gonzo. "We don't really know them."

"We know they need our help," the grasshopper replied.

"Yes," said Zap, "but what if—"

"We can't be suspicious of everyone," interrupted Gonzo, "especially when babies are at risk."

Zap lowered his head, feeling bad about not wanting to help. *If Gonzo trusts them, then so will I.*

The Bug Buddies and the tiger beetles gathered around the grasshopper.

"Right," said Gonzo. "I know just the place for the eggs – Mud Valley. The ground there is soft enough to dig tunnels quickly."

"Isn't that a bit close to Shadow Creek?" Crunch asked.

"So what?" said Lurch. "That's a spider-free zone now!"

"You'll have to move quickly," said Gonzo. "There's a storm coming. I'm putting Zap in charge of leading the way. I must stay here in case any other bugs need my help."

Zap felt proud. This was an

important mission – they couldn't let
Gonzo and the tiger beetles down.

The sky darkened as Zap led the
long crawl over to Mud Valley. The
Bug Buddies helped Snap and his
friends roll the eggs gently along the
ground. The windy weather blew the

eggs off course, making it hard work and they had to keep scampering around to stop the eggs rolling away completely.

Zap smiled when he noticed that Lurch was pushing two eggs at once. "You're doing a great job there," he said.

"I knew all that poo-rolling would come in handy one day!" Lurch replied.

Fat, grey clouds rolled across the sky. The storm was going to break any moment now. Zap was relieved when they reached the brown banks of Mud Valley.

"We're here," he said, stopping to catch his breath.

Snap immediately began to burrow into the soil, searching for the softest ground to dig. Zap was impressed by the way Snap threw

himself into the work. *He really cares about those babies,* he thought.

Then Lurch noticed a hole in the muddy bank.

"Look," he said, pointing his leg. "Someone's already started a tunnel."

Snap crawled over to examine the hole. "Great," he said. "This should

save us lots of time."

Lurch bent close to the ground
and followed a scent he'd picked up.
He scuttled to the edge of the hole

 and held up a
small ball of poo,
examining it
carefully. "Mouse
droppings," he said.

"Mice must have been searching
for food here."

"Well, they're gone now," said Snap.
"Come on, tiger beetles. Let's burrow!"

The tiger beetles placed the eggs

under a bush near the hole. They then set to work making the hole bigger, as a loud clap of thunder boomed across the sky.

"I h-hate thunder," said Crunch, quivering. "Can we go home now?"

Zap looked at the dark clouds above. The tiger beetles were burrowing as fast as they could, but the storm was nearly upon them.

"Not yet," said Zap. "We can't abandon bugs in need. The tunnel will be dug much quicker if we all help."

The Bug Buddies rushed forward to help out too. Now there was one giant team burrowing into the ground together, trying to make a home big enough for the tiger beetle family. Zap carried lumps of dirt away from the hole, while Crunch used his claws to move huge chunks of earth.

"I never knew I was so good at digging," said Crunch proudly. Deeper and deeper

they dug into the cold, dark
earth. The thunder was
followed by lightning and
then the steady drip, drip,
drip of rain.

The storm had arrived.

Zap's legs tingled with
nerves as the rain got
heavier and began to pour
down the tunnel.

"The hole isn't big
enough," shouted Crunch.
"The rain is going to fill it up!"

Zap flicked water off his wings.

Could they dig fast enough to save the eggs from the downpour?

CHAPTER 4

The Bug Buddies worked harder
than ever. Zap whizzed out of the
tunnel, struggling to hold on to a
lump of dirt. A huge raindrop
smacked into his body, sending him
plummeting to the ground.

Zap stumbled back to his feet and

shook himself dry. *It'll take more than rain to stop me,* he thought. He was about to fly back to get some more soil when he heard a loud **CRACK!**

What was that?

Snap rushed out of the tunnel.

"Oh no," cried Snap. **"The eggs are about to hatch!"**

He was right – Zap could see a few of the eggs starting to split.

There was a muffled sound of cheering from the tunnel. Zap zoomed

back underground, with Snap flying
just ahead of him. He turned a
corner to see that Crunch had
knocked down a whole side wall of
earth, revealing a large tunnel with
two smaller tunnels shooting off
from it further down.

"Well done, Crunch!" cried Zap.

"I just need to check that the walls of the largest tunnel are strong enough," said Snap.

He crawled forward and tapped the ceiling of the largest tunnel with his front leg, listening closely to the sound it made. "We'll be fine here," he said with relief.

"Time to get the eggs," said Zap. Then a thought popped into his head. *Who had built these tunnels? And where were they now?*

But his friends were already

crawling back to the surface.

The bugs gently rolled the eggs underground, being careful not to crack them even more.

Once all the eggs were safely inside, the Bug Buddies each took one between their feet and began to roll the eggs into the large tunnel. It was pitch black.

"I can't even see my front legs!" cried Lurch.

"How can we get light so deep underground?" said Snap.

Then Zap had a brainwave.

"I know a family of fireflies who live nearby," he said. "I'll go and ask them if they will light up the tunnel." Zap soared back towards the surface. "I'll fly as fast as I can," he shouted. "Even if it's not as fast as a tiger beetle," he added under his breath.

Zap found the fireflies sheltering under an oak leaf. When he explained what he needed them to do, they shook their heads, frightened. "What if I promise that you can play the Bug Buddies at Beetle Ball tomorrow?" Zap bargained.

"Deal!" they said.

The fireflies followed Zap into
the hole and flew down the large
tunnel. The warm, yellow glow from
their bodies filled it with light.

"Hooray," cried Lurch. "We can see!"

Zap and his friends rolled the eggs deep into the large tunnel.

"That's far enough," said Snap. "All we have to do now is wait for the storm to pass."

The tiger beetles scuttled forward and stood shoulder to shoulder, forming a protective circle around their eggs.

Zap watched through the gaps between beetles as the eggs began to hatch. One after another, baby tiger beetles emerged from their shells. It was amazing – they looked like miniature, see-through copies of Snap! Zap smiled as one started crawling towards him, wobbling on its tiny legs. But his smile soon faded when the baby snapped its jaws

together hungrily. Zap scuttled
backwards, feeling slightly afraid.

Snap gently placed a leg in front
of the young beetle, barring its way.

"Want food!" squeaked the baby,
still moving its legs, but not getting
anywhere.

"Well this weevil over here is
NOT for eating," said Snap loudly to
all the babies, pointing at Zap.
"Sorry," he apologised, "it's in their
nature to hunt weevils. We'll teach
them who their friends are."

Zap nodded. *I was right to trust*

Snap, he thought.

Suddenly, something shiny and white shot out from the darkness. Zap gasped as a silky strand wrapped around a newly-hatched tiger beetle and started to drag it further into the shadowy tunnel.

"Watch out," yelled Zap.

CHAPTER 5

The baby tiger beetle was being
dragged into the shadows.

Zap knew they had to do
something quickly. "Please fly further
down the tunnel," he said to the
fireflies, "so we can see what we're
dealing with."

The fireflies flew on and Zap
followed. The yellow light of the
fireflies cast a shadow on the tunnel
wall. Zap held his breath as one,
two, then… *eight* thick legs appeared
on the muddy wall.

The shadow began to move, as giant hairy legs covered in dried flecks of honey appeared out of the darkness, followed by a huge black body. **Spinner!**

Zap's wings quivered as the evil spider grinned at him.

"Surprise!" cried Spinner.

I was right, thought Zap. *Spinner has been hiding out all this time, right under our feet!*

"W-W-Who's that?" asked Snap, his voice wobbling.

"The most evil spider ever!" said Zap.

"I don't understand," shouted Lurch. "We saw you fall into the honey lake."

"Stupid bugs," laughed Spinner.

59

"It'll take more than honey to defeat me!"

The giant spider continued pulling the silky thread towards him. The baby tiger beetle was getting closer and closer to his sharp fangs.

"And," cried Spinner, "after I've had this little snack, I'll be filling myself up on the famous Bug Buddies!"

"Not if we've got anything to do with it," shouted Zap. He turned quickly to his friends. "Buzz and Lurch, lead the other bugs out

to ground level," he whispered.
"Crunch, I'll distract Spinner while
you use your antlers to cut the baby
free."

"OK," said Crunch, nodding
nervously.

Zap whizzed down
the tunnel towards
the evil spider. He
hovered right in
front of
Spinner's face
and wiggled his
antennae at him.

"If you want to eat me," he teased, "you've got to catch me first!"

Zap heard Spinner growl angrily and start after him as he zoomed away.

"Get a move on, Crunch!" he shouted, as his friend cut through the silky strands to free the tiger beetle. Crunch scooped the baby

beetle up in his giant claws.

"You're safe now, little one," he said, carrying him away.

"Why, you **sneaky beetles!**" cried Spinner.

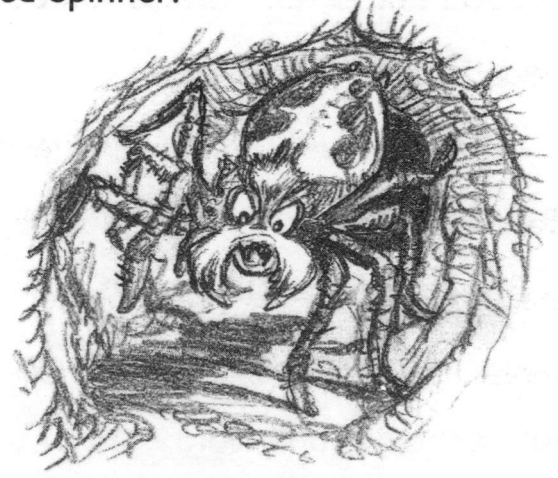

The spider had crawled after Zap as fast as he could, but it was difficult for him to move quickly in

such a small space. For once, Zap
had size on his side! He landed next
to his friends at the entrance to the
two smaller tunnels.

"Right," he said, "everyone up to
the surface!"

"And keep your antennae crossed
that the storm is over," said Snap.

But before the bugs could crawl
away, two more silk threads shot
out at them – one from each of the
smaller tunnels. Each thread
wrapped around a baby beetle,
trapping two more.

"**Oh no,**" cried Lurch. "**More spiders!**"

The fireflies lit up the two small tunnels that the trapped baby tiger beetles were being dragged down. At the end of each tunnel was a spider: smaller than Spinner, but with the same hungry eyes.

Zap's heart thudded. *Three spiders?* How could they battle them all?

CHAPTER 6

Crunch leapt forward and sliced both of the silky strands. The two spiders retreated into the darkness as Crunch guided the babies to safety.

"Well done," said Zap, smiling at his brave friend.

"I hate it when big bugs pick on

little bugs," said Crunch, puffing and panting.

"What are we going to do?" said Snap. "Those spiders are just going to keep on coming."

"I don't think Spinner's going anywhere for a while," said Lurch.

Zap looked round to see that Spinner was in the largest tunnel. The giant spider had managed to push his way in there, but he was too big to get out.

"Help me!" cried Spinner, desperately.

"No way," said Zap. "But thanks,
Spinner – you've just given me an
idea."

He turned back to his friends.
There was no time to lose!

"We need to block these tunnels
so that the spiders can't get out," he
said. "Snap, you and the tiger
beetles can push mud to block up
Spinner's tunnel and trap him inside.
The fireflies will make sure you have
enough light to see."

"Great idea," said Snap, quickly
waving the babies out of the way.

Then the tiger beetles set to work, shovelling dirt forward.

"What about the smaller tunnels?" asked Buzz.

"Crunch could go down that one and scare the spider away," said Lurch.

"OK," said Crunch. "I'll try." He took a deep breath and puffed out his chest, muttering to himself, "Remember, you hate bullies!"

He charged into the tunnel on the right and shook his antlers at the spider, who quickly backed off.

"There's one tunnel left," said Buzz. "But Snap is using all the spare mud to trap Spinner. What shall we do?"

"Poo!" shouted Lurch.

"Not now," said Buzz. "Wait until we get outside!"

"I didn't mean that," said Lurch. "Why don't I fly out and get the mouse droppings? I can roll them into a great big dung ball to block

up the last tunnel."

"Brilliant," said Zap. "It'll be quicker if Buzz helps you."

The ladybird wrinkled up his nose, disgusted. "OK," he mumbled, crawling after Lurch. "But sometimes, I really wish you weren't a dung beetle!"

With all his friends busy, it was down to Zap to lead the babies to safety. The spiders were being kept

at bay, but he knew that might not last long.

Zap flew over to the baby tiger beetles and hovered in the air. "OK, guys," he said. "You need to follow me, flying as fast and high as you can."

"But we can't fly yet," said the babies. "We haven't learned how to."

Oh no, thought Zap. *How am I going to get them out?*

CHAPTER 7

There was only one thing for it.

"Forget about flying," Zap said.
"Let's all *crawl* as fast as we can."

Zap scurried up the tunnel at
double-quick speed. He looked
behind him to make sure the babies
were keeping up. But they were still

standing right where he'd left them.

They were too terrified to move!

I know, thought Zap, heading back
to them, *I'll turn it into a game.*

"How about I teach you a
marching song?" said Zap.

He began to sing:

One, two, three, four,

Bugs are crawling on the floor,

Five, six, seven, eight,

Better be quick, 'cos we won't wait.

The babies jumped up and down,
singing along. Soon, they were

marching right behind Zap.

After crawling up the slippery
brown tunnel, Zap and the babies
finally made it back above ground. He
lifted the little beetles on to the grass,
relieved to see that the storm had
passed completely. The grey clouds

had been replaced by a blue sky.

"Now stay here while I go and fetch Snap," Zap told the babies.

Zap flew back into the tunnel. But as he flew down through the main entrance, he saw the fireflies and the tiger beetles flying up towards him. Zap had to dodge out of the way as they all came zooming out.

"What's happened?" he asked.

"Spinner's broken out," said Snap, breathlessly. **"He's coming this way!"**

Zap's tummy did a nervous flip. Where were the rest of the Bug Buddies?

Zap whizzed underground and began searching for his friends. He zipped down the dark tunnel and spotted Buzz, Lurch and Crunch being chased by Spinner.

"This way!" shouted Zap.

The Bug Buddies hurried towards him, kicking mud backwards to try and keep Spinner at bay.

"You head to the surface," said Zap. "Leave Spinner to me."

"But—" said Buzz.

"Trust me," said Zap.

Buzz, Crunch and Lurch scrambled away, leaving Zap face to face with Spinner.

"What's this?" said Spinner, smiling. "Decided to let me eat you after all?"

Zap flapped his wings defiantly.

"The only thing you'll be eating is a mouthful of mud!"

Spinner hissed and scuttled towards him. Zap dodged past Spinner and into the tunnel to the left. But as he zoomed along, he realised he'd made a terrible mistake.

It was a dead end and one of the smaller spiders was coming towards him!

"Finally," hissed Spinner.

"There's no escape."

As Zap edged back from the advancing spider, venom dripped

from Spinner's fangs. He crouched
down preparing to bite, when Zap
spotted a chink of light out of the
corner of his eye. There was a small
hole in the tunnel's ceiling. It was too
small for the spiders to get through!

Zap flew up and squeezed his tiny body through the hole. **"No!"** shouted Spinner from the tunnel below, as Zap pushed himself up through the mud.

The hole was so tight, Zap couldn't breathe. *Oh no, I'm going to get stuck,* he thought. Before his breath ran out, he gave one last big push. He slipped through the mud and burst out on to the surface next to a chestnut tree.

He'd escaped from Spinner!

CHAPTER 8

"Hooray!" cheered Lurch, crawling over to Zap. "You're safe!"

Just as the tiger beetles came to join them, there was a rustling sound from above. Zap looked up to see Crunch shaking a branch with his claws. A conker fell off and smashed

into the main entrance to the
tunnels. Now there was no
way in and no way out.

"Those spider bullies
will be stuck down there
now," shouted Crunch.

Suddenly, they heard a

muffled voice from below ground.

"I'll be back!" yelled Spinner.

And I'll be ready for you, Zap
thought.

Back on Gonzo's Rock, the
grasshopper listened as Zap, Buzz,
Lurch and Crunch told the story of
their near miss with Spinner and the
daring rescue.

"You are some brave bugs," said
Snap.

"I agree," said Gonzo. "You
defended the babies and outwitted

84

Spinner by working as a team. And
Zap, you led the babies to safety
then went back to save your friends.
You've been a real hero today."

Zap felt his cheeks getting hot.

"And," Gonzo continued, "you did it all without relying on your speed."

"I wasn't the only one who used other skills," said Zap, smiling at the Bug Buddies.

Suddenly, he felt a gentle tug on his wing. Zap looked down to see

the baby tiger beetles crowded around him.

"Can we play the marching game again?" asked one of them, with a hopeful glint in his eye.

"OK," said Zap, looking at the tiger beetles. "But there's something I need to say to you all first... Welcome to Spinner's Wood!"

"Thank you," said Snap. "I think we're going to be very happy here."

As the Bug Buddies marched along with the babies, Zap knew Snap was right. There was no better

place to be a bug. He wouldn't want
to live anywhere else. And though
he may not be the fastest bug in
Spinner's Wood now, he was still
more than a match for Spinner.

Zap would be ready to face that
wicked spider the next time he
launched an attack. And he knew
one thing for certain. With that
nasty spider there would *always* be a
next time...

DUNG BEETLE

NAME: Lurch

FAMILY: Scarabaeidae

SIZE: 2 cm

HOME: the stinkiest parts
of Spinner's Wood

LIKES: fresh poo, rolling dung
balls

DISLIKES: cobwebs, dung ball
thieves

LURCH

Dung beetles bury nearly half a ton of dung per acre per year as food!

There are around 7000 different species of dung beetle, and many specialise in different kinds of dung. That's a lot of beetles and a lot of poo!

Dung Beetles live in every continent except Antarctica. That's over a thousand species per continent!

BUG BUDDIES

Beetle Power!

Even beetles can be heroes

BUG BUDDIES

JOE MILLER

Beetle Power!

It's the final showdown with Spinner. If he's defeated, he'll be banished forever!

COMING SOON!

Turn over for a sneak preview of book five...

Zap saw Buzz sitting on a rock which was covered in small, black spots.

"Time to play a trick," said Zap, mischievously.

Zap, Lurch and Crunch flew across the pond, landing next to Buzz.

"Oh no," said Zap, pointing at the rock, "are you losing your spots?"

Buzz spat out his snack. "My spots! Pick them up, quick!" he cried and started scrabbling around on the rock.

"I'm only teasing," said Zap. "Your spots can't really fall off.

Anyway, you don't have this many. You've only got seven, remember?"

Lurch scuttled across the rock, examining the dark spots with a worried expression on his face.

"What's wrong?" asked Zap.

"We'd better be on the lookout for more of these," said Lurch.

"Why?" asked Crunch. "They're just a bunch of spots."

"Depends on who left them here," said Lurch.

To be continued...

BUG BUDDIES

JOE MILLER

Buy more great Bug Buddies books direct from
HarperCollins *Publishers*: at 10% off recommended
retail price. FREE postage and packing in the UK.

The Big Game	ISBN: 978-0-00-731039-5
Enemy Attack!	ISBN: 978-0-00-731040-1
Ant Invasion!	ISBN: 978-0-00-731041-8
Tunnel Trouble	ISBN: 978-0-00-731042-5

All priced at £3.99 RRP

More books coming soon!

| Beetle Power! | ISBN: 978-0-00-732247-3 |
| Slime Time | ISBN: 978-0-00-732248-0 |